The Plot Against the King

The Plot Against the King

Written by: Kash Patel

Art by: Laura Vincent

Once upon a time, in the Land of the Free, there lived a wizard called Kash the Distinguished Discoverer.

Kash was known far and wide as the one person who could discover anything about anything. He found the Holy Grape, deep in the Enchanted Forest, and he discovered who had stolen the sleeping princess.

The heralds, who spread important news across the land with their herald trumpets, had sung of Kash's fame ever since he figured out that the Russionians were cheating in the jousting tournaments.

But all these quests had been easy for Kash, and as the sun rose and set over the Land of the Free, Kash found himself in grave danger, not of trolls or ogres, but of getting bored.

That is, until the Choosing Day.

On Choosing Day the whole land gathered at the castle to choose the next ruler of the kingdom. The heralds had been announcing that Hillary Queenton would be queen. She says queenly things like *thee* and *thou* and *forsooth*, and her last name *is* Queenton, after all.

But when the royal counter-uppers counted up the final votes, they realized the people had dared to choose the merchant Donald! The heralds and Hillary were horrified. Donald didn't care what the heralds said about him, and he was determined to Make the Kingdom Great Again.

Thus, King Donald moved into the castle, and everyone turned to head home.

But before the people could leave, a herald jumped onto his stand to make a proclamation. "Wait!" he proclaimed through his herald trumpet. "Listen to what this noble knight has to say."

Then a shifty-looking knight jumped onto the stand. "Donald isn't the rightful king. Inside this steel box, I have found a paper that says Donald cheated his way to the throne!"

All of the people gasped. "We're shocked! How could he do such a thing?"

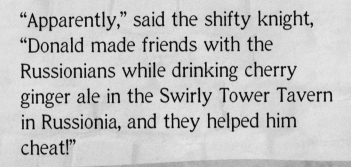

"Apparently," said the shifty knight, "Donald made friends with the Russionians while drinking cherry ginger ale in the Swirly Tower Tavern in Russionia, and they helped him cheat!"

All of the people nodded. "The heralds must be right. After all, they have loud trumpets and important pieces of paper. King Donald must be a cheater."

And so, even though they hadn't looked at all the facts, everyone agreed that King Donald was a cheater—everyone except for Duke Devin, of the King's court.

Duke Devin had known Donald for years, and he couldn't imagine the King had cheated. The Duke was loyal to the core, which is why Kash was not at all surprised when he walked through Kash's front door.

"Kash!" said the distressed duke. "I am distressed. I know these terrible, tragical, tangle-full rumors cannot be true of King Donald, but the heralds keep saying that they are true! It must be a plot against the king."

"That's a very serious thing to say," said Kash seriously. "What does King Donald think about all this?"

"He calls them all fake heralds," shrugged the Duke, "but I must know what really happened."

"We can't decide if they're right or wrong until we know all the facts, and if you're looking for facts, you came to the right place." Kash put on his wizard hat. "I am the Distinguished Discoverer, so I can discover anything about anything. I'll help you—on one condition: I must share the truth with everyone, no matter what I find."

"Of course," said Duke Devin. And so they set out on *The Quest for the Truth about the Plot against the King*.

For their first stop, Kash and Devin visited the shifty knight and his herald friends. "I'm absolutely sure that Sir Trump is a cheater!" the shifty knight said. "I found the paper that proves it right here, in this steel box." But when Kash looked into the box, he found a long, sticky, silvery streak of slime.

"Ah," said Devin. "I've seen this before." He and Kash hurried to the slug stables in a shadowy corner of the castle.

The keeper of the slugs, named Keeper Komey, was in charge of delivering all the king's secret messages. But on his desk, Kash spotted a suspicious letter.

Dear Komey,

Most sincerely, I thank thee for the service of delivering my papers with thine slugs to the steel box so sneakily. Forsooth! In all the land, shall not be found a deceiver so daring or so devious.

All my love,

Hillary Queenton

"Aha!" cried Kash. "Now we know where the mysterious rumor came from. All we have left is to discover whether or not Hillary Queenton is lying."

That very evening, Kash and Devin set off for the kingdom of Russionia to seek the Swirly Tower Tavern, but when they arrived there was no such place to be found! They searched and searched. They looked around all the corners and in all the cracks. They even asked the locals, who only huffed and grunted and couldn't help at all. No one had ever heard of such a place.

"I've discovered," said Kash, "that the Swirly Tower Tavern cannot be discovered. The steel box paper is looking very suspicious."

"It only makes sense," said Duke Devin. "Everyone knows King Donald doesn't even drink cherry ginger ale."

Kash and Duke Devin hurried back to the Land of the Free, straight to the king's castle. They had an important meeting to call.

All of the heralds and all of the knights filed into the room. The shifty knight stood at the very front.

Kash declared, "The steel box paper is not true—we went to Russionia, and we discovered there is no Swirly Tower Tavern! So now I need to know, do any of you have any other reason to believe King Donald cheated in any way?"

One by one, they all scratched their heads and cleared their throats and said, "No, no. I don't know of any reason or any way."

Afterwards, Kash followed the shifty knight outside. "If you didn't have a reason to believe that King Donald was a cheater, why did you say all those nasty things about him to the heralds?"

"We tried our best to find evidence. Keeper Komey even sent his slugs into the castle to spy on the king. But I don't care that we couldn't find anything." The shifty knight shifted. "I just really don't like Donald."

Then the shifty knight ran straight to the heralds. "Heralds!" he said. "Go forth throughout the kingdom! I have a very good reason to believe that King Donald is a cheater."

"What is it?" the heralds asked.

"I can't tell you; it's a secret," the shifty knight smiled.

"Oooh," said the heralds. They all loved secrets. "We'll tell everyone right away." And so they did.

All of the people nodded when they heard. "They must be right. After all, they have loud trumpets and an important secret." And so, everyone agreed that the shifty knight was telling the truth, even though they didn't have any reason to believe him.

As he watched all of this happen, the king became sad. "They're still spreading lies," he told Kash. "How will the people ever learn the truth?" Kash sighed. He knew the answer. It was up to him to present the evidence to the people.

Gathering his courage and all of his evidence, Kash dashed up the stairs that wound around the Gold Tower, but Hillary and the shifty knight were right behind him.

When Kash reached the top, he paused to tie his wizard shoes. Unfortunately, Hillary and the shifty knight didn't see him stop, and they tumbled over him.

Kash stood up and addressed everybody. "Everybody! I am Kash, the Great Wizard and the Distinguished Discoverer. I have discovered that the king, King Donald, is innocent! He did not work with the Russionians, and he did not cheat. You chose him, so he became king, fair and square.

Hillary wrote that paper and had her sneaky slugs slide it into the steel box for the shifty knight to find.

Now that you know more of the facts, it's time for you to think carefully and decide what you think of the king. Don't just trust the person with the loudest trumpet."

The people paused and considered Kash's speech. "Ah, we shouldn't have believed that the King was a cheater without any proof," they said. Now that they had all the evidence, they clapped and cheered and threw a huge party for their king.

The shifty knight tried to say Kash was lying, but the Knights of the Oval Table carried him, Hillary Queenton, and Keeper Komey out of the kingdom, banishing them forever.

Some of the heralds kept spreading the rumor, but they soon grew bored. They moved on to more exciting tales, declaring the sun was made of mustard and would soon drip down and make everything yellow and mustardy.

Kash only shrugged. As long as there were people in the Land of the Free, someone would be trying to spread a ridiculous story. But Kash was satisfied that he knew the truth, and after his proclamation, anyone else who wanted to know what really happened could learn it, too.

And so, Duke Devin, King Donald, and Kash the Distinguished Discoverer went back into the castle to share a nice meal with no cherry ginger ale.

With that, the Kingdom was Made Great Again, and from that day on, they lived happily ever after.

THE END

The true story of Kash Patel and Russiagate.

Dear Citizen of the Land of Opportunity,

After Donald Trump's election in 2016, the liberal media began buzzing about a leaked document known as the Steele Dossier. Written by Christopher Steele, the dossier claimed that President Trump had colluded with Russia to steal the election.

The House Permanent Select Committee on Intelligence was chosen to investigate this "Russia collusion narrative," and Chairman Devin Nunes asked me, Kash Patel, to lead his team. We conducted our investigation in three steps:

- First, we fact checked the dossier and found significant evidence that several incriminating details could not be accurate.

- Second, we followed the money back to the organization that had paid Steele for his report: the Hillary Clinton Campaign and the Democratic National Committee.

- Third, we interrogated over 60 witnesses under oath, none of whom could affirmatively say they had proof that Trump or his administration colluded, conspired, or coordinated with Russia. While our investigative hearings were still in process, many of these witnesses claimed the exact opposite to the mainstream media.

The leader of the only false narrative to come out of Russiagate was Adam Schiff, who earned a reputation for promising the media that he had the scoop on how Trump had colluded with Russia—except he couldn't share because it was "classified."

Devin and I published our findings in the Nunes Memo and declassified the Department of Justice and the FBI's own documents. Immediately, Schiff responded with one meritless claim after another. The mainstream media lapped it up. His own Schiff Memo was lauded by journalists who seemed to be only looking for the next flashy headline, whether or not it was true.

In the years since, it's been a slow and steady fight for justice. Former FBI director James Comey, his Deputy Andy McCabe, and fifteen

others were fired or resigned for their involvement in misleading a federal court to get surveillance warrants of Trump World (which were later vacated as a result of our investigation). And in the time since, the Inspector General of DOJ, the Attorney General, and the FBI director all under oath admitted Hillary and the DNC did pay Steele for his dossier and intentionally misled the court just to investigate a political opponent they never wanted to see in the White House.

This book is one way I'm doing my part to share the truth. This story cannot be forgotten. I also had the honor of contributing to a documentary, *The Plot Against the President*, where Devin, Donald Trump, Jr, and I, along with several others, told our story in much more detail. I hope you'll do research for yourself so that you can learn the truth about this plot against the king.

Blessings,

Kash Patel

@Kash on Truth Social

fightwithkash.com